This is a Borzoi Book published by Alfred A. Knopf, a division of Random House, Inc.

Copyright © 1999, 2001 by Hachette Livre
All rights reserved under International and Pan-American Copyright
Conventions. Published in the United States of America by Alfred A. Knopf,
a division of Random House, Inc., New York, and simultaneously in Canada by
Random House of Canada Limited, Toronto. Distributed by Random House, Inc.,
New York. Originally published in France as Gaspard à Venise
by Hachette Jeunesse in 1999. KNOPF, BORZOI BOOKS, and the colophon
are registered trademarks of Random House, Inc.
www.randomhouse.com/kids
Library of Congress Catalog Card Number: 00-131161

ISBN 0-375-81115-X

First Borzoi Books edition: March 2001

Printed in France

10 9 8 7 6 5 4 3 2

ANNE GUTMAN

Gaspard on Vacation

GEORG HALLENSLEBEN

Alfred

I'm Gaspard. I love to travel, and guess where I went for my vacation?

Venice! With my whole family—my parents, my brother, and even my baby sister, Louise.

And what do you think we
did from morning to night?

We went to museums.

Museums, museums, and more museums. Just as we were about to go into another museum,

I saw a little red kayak just my size, and...

...I took off!

I paddled along small canals and...

...big canals.

I had a lot of fun
and explored everywhere.
Maybe I was going too fast,
but suddenly—

CRASH! SPLASH!
I had an accident. I was
lucky, but the people in
the big black gondola
fell into the water.

Boy, were
they angry!

So I paddled faster...   and faster...

and even faster...   until I was too tired to go on.

Then I hid behind a curtain in front of a church door. It was getting dark. I wondered if my parents missed me. I was a little bit scared.

Especially when I saw the police boat with the big searchlight. It was coming straight toward me.

What would the police do to me?

But my parents were
with them! And they
weren't even angry.
They were so happy to
have found me.

To celebrate, we went to a restaurant and had the best spaghetti in the world. "Tomorrow, we're all going on a gondola ride," said Dad, "and I hope there won't be any little rascals in kayaks."